If you're lonely
If you're horny
Perhaps a little bored
Cum to the darkest place in town
The little shop
little shop of sex toys
There are no windows
And a door small enough to poke your head in
Quick
Quick
Shut the door
shut the door
Don't let the musk out
Musk out
Cum to the darkest place in town
The little shop
little shop of sex toys
Cum for the fun
No matter your kink
No matter your pleasure
Tie me up

Lay me down
Fill my voids
Cum to the darkest place in town
The little shop
little shop of sex toys
lube me up
lick me down
make me sweat
Vibrate, vibrate, vibrate

Cover by RuthAnna Evans

Wacky John

Eady H

Published by Eady H, 2024.

This is a work of fiction. Similarities to real people, places, or events are entirely coincidental.

WACKY JOHN

First edition. March 13, 2024.

Copyright © 2024 Eady H.

ISBN: 979-8224809912

Written by Eady H.

On the corner of fifth and vine sits the little shop of sex toys. It's a square brick structure on a lonely street full of broken buildings. The sign on the outside of the shop is missing several of its bulbs, but despite its decrepit appearance it is the only source of sexual sin in town. And I mean that in the best way possible. The town is too small for prostitutes, so the residents are left with renting blow up dolls from the little shop of sex toys. And while the shop has several to choose from, Rebecca is the favorite.

On this wintry day Jonathan slips into the dimly lit shop seeking the comfort of Rebecca. Like everyone else, she's his favorite blow-up doll but sometimes there's a wait list for her.

He loves her so much he's the one that named her and even graffitied her name across her chest. A little mark he'd given her to claim a piece of her as his. Real classy guy that Jonathan. Today is his lucky day. His name is at the top of the wait list for Rebecca.

He accepts her gingerly from the cashier and carries her outside like a husband carries his wife across the threshold when they marry then places her in the front seat of his car and buckles her in. "We're going to have so much fun, Rebecca," he says.

Jonathan takes the driver's seat and grabs Rebecca's hand while he drives. He wants to keep her forever, but he knows he only has the night to live his fantasy. She's just so pretty and everything he wants in a woman. His thumb strokes her hand absentmindedly until he pulls up in front of his apartment. After parking he looks around to make sure no one is looking before he helps Rebecca from the car and carries her to his apartment on the second floor.

Jonathan doesn't waste any time as he takes her directly to the bedroom and lays her on his bed. He slides in beside her and lays his head on her tits then slides his hand across her forehead like he's smoothing hair from her face.

Just imagine if you were real
I'd lick your nipples and play with your hair
Just imagine me inside your warmth
Just imagine
Just imagine
Oh, Rebecca my love
What we could do if you were real
While away the day in bed
Share a meal
Share a laugh
Share a life
Just imagine if you could carry my child
I'd be the perfect husband
If you'd be my wife
Just imagine if you could grow old with me
Decompose with me
Just imagine
Just imagine
Oh, Rebecca my love
What we could do if you were real
Heavenly stars above

Look upon us with pity
If I had one wish
She'd be made of flesh
No more lonely nights
If she was my wife
Oh Rebecca

But the stars do not look on him with pity. They look on Jonathan with fuck around and find out energy. As he falls asleep after their post coital activities, Rebecca turns her head and looks at him.

The sheets are weird against her skin. Oh my god she's got skin. She can hear noises and they're overwhelming her. Her ears work? A light comes through the window right in her face and she squints. *What the hell is going on?* She blinks once and screams bloody murder.

Jonathan shoots out of the bed and gapes at her. She runs her hands down her body with a disgusted face as she touches his cum coating her.

"What the fuck," Jonathan says.

The stars are laughing now as his wish moves before him, disgusted by her situation.

"Ewwwwww. What the hell is this?"

"My uh cum. How are you alive?"

"How are you alive?" she snaps shaking her hands and slinging his cum. It slaps the wall with a nasty sound.

"I was born. Oh my god, I wished you alive. I asked the stars to bring you to life." He moves back to sit next to her on the bed.

"Why?"

He takes her gingerly in his arms and she stiffens. "To be my partner. My wife. My love."

As a former blow-up doll these concepts are meaningless to Rebecca. All she's ever been shown is lust. But where else can she go. She knows nothing of the world.

"Come, let's get you clean. While you shower, I will run out and buy you some clothes."

Jonathan leads Rebecca into the shower then leaves. She luxuriates in the feel of hot water on her new skin. She's been sanitized lots of times, but never bathed. She stays there until the water cools.

When Jonathan comes back, she is standing at the window wearing a towel. Her hair is damp and hangs down her back. He runs his fingers across it as he moves to stand behind her. He sets his chin on her shoulder for a moment, and they look out the window together, his hands around her stomach.

"I got you some nice things," he says as he turns her toward the bed.

A large black bag sits on it. Jonathan leads her over and gestures for her to sit on it. He pulls lingerie pieces from it and shows them to her with childlike excitement.

"You'll be stunning in this," he says.

Rebecca thinks she might as well just be naked, but Jonathan looks so happy with his purchases, so she says nothing. He picks out what he calls a nighty, and she slips it on. He tugs her into his arms as he lays down and soon, he's snoring in her ear as she lays awake staring at the ceiling. If this is life she might have preferred being a mindless doll. She feels like nothing has changed in her situation except now she's breathing.

In the morning Jonathan gets ready for work then turns his tv to the cooking channel. "I'll be home around five thirty if you'd have dinner ready honey." He kisses her forehead then leaves.

Rebecca goes back to bed and finally let's sleep claim her. When she wakes Jonathan is home and standing at the foot of the bed. He looks pissed with his hands on his hips staring at her.

"Where is dinner?"

"In the cabinet probably." She doesn't know how to fucking cook. Jesus she's been alive less than a full day.

"I asked you to have dinner ready when I got home. I've been working all day. Have you been in bed this whole time."

The tone of his voice pisses her off. Like he thinks she's lazy. "You snore. How was I supposed to sleep through that?"

Jonathan huffs. "I'll order pizza tonight, but tomorrow there better be dinner."

"Uh huh." Like she'd know how to cook any better tomorrow. She was created for one thing. Sex.

After pizza Jonathan fucks Rebecca leaving her sticky once more. And so, the days go. She tries to cook him dinner sometimes and he fucks her leaving her a mess. While he's gone during the day she watches cooking shows and a movie called Stepford Wives. And she longs for more. But she knows Jonathan will never let her go. Will never let her be more than a house and bed slave.

He constantly touches her when he's home and she finds she's touched out. She prefers daytime when he's gone and she's alone. She finds herself staring out the window for long periods of time. The mood in the apartment makes her depressed.

While he sleeps, she stares out the window at the stars above. The same stars that brought her to life and she sees them smile at her. He'd fucked around and now it was time for him to find out.

Oh god, I'm sticky again
Feeling used and filthy
Tired of being a doll
I'm real
I'm real
So tired of being sticky
So tired of playing pretend
My reality is hell to your heaven
Let this end
You promised a partnership
But you made a Stepford wife
A perfect doll here to please
You baste me in your juices
Slather me with your sticky ickies
What about my needs
So tired of being sticky
So tired of playing pretend
My reality is hell to your heaven
Let this end
I'm wet again but not for you
I get more pleasure from myself

I hope your balls turn blue
And your dick falls limp
So tired of being sticky
So tired of playing pretend
My reality is hell to your heaven
This will end

Rebecca climbs on top of Jonathan and presses a pillow to his face. He squirms under her, and she presses harder, but he's stronger than her. He thrusts his hips up and topples her then wrenches the pillow off his face and kicks Rebecca so hard she crashes out the window and lands on the lawn two stories down. As she flies out the window she yells 'so long and thanks for all the semen.'

The wind is knocked out of her as she slams into the ground and gasps. She sees Jonathan looking down at her from the broken window.

"I gave you everything!" he yells.

"Except an orgasm," Rebecca yells back then rolls over and gets to her feet. She limps out of his view and starts down the sidewalk. One of her heels is missing and her steps are uneven. She's elated to find herself free from Jonathan. Though she has no idea where to go or what to do.

Jonathan places his palm against the window and watches the perfect woman hobble out of his life into the cold night. Perhaps the fault for her exit was in him. Maybe he hadn't explained exactly what was expected of her as a perfect mate. But already his home feels emptier, and loneliness consumes him. Instead of sadness though he feels anger at his loneliness. He'd given her the gift of life and she'd spurned him. What kinda bitch?

What kinda bitch
Can't
Service in the bedroom
Jonathan throws her lingerie out the broken
window. The breeze catches them and blows
them away as he moves to the kitchen.
Can't
Feed a man
He swipes dirty dishes off the counter and
they clatter to the floor.
Should've loved me
Should've stayed
Ain't a real woman anyway
What kind of bitch
What kind of bitch
That fake ass bitch
Bitch
A woman belongs in
The kitchen
In the bedroom
Keep your mouth closed

Especially around my dick
What kind of bitch
What kind of bitch
That fake ass bitch
Bitch
Make me a sandwich
Make me a baby
You're so pretty when you smile
What kind of bitch
What kind of bitch
That fake ass bitch
Bitch
Bow down bitch
Bow down

Jonathan storms out of his apartment. His anger at Rebecca growing. He was going to take away the only thing she had.

Rebecca wanders the cold dark streets. Her outfit doesn't leave much to the imagination and she shivers in the frigid air. She has nowhere to go and no money to survive. Jonathan never let her touch the money. She only got what he provided for her.

Her steps lead her back to the little shop of sex toys. Her home. Granted a home she didn't remember because a plastic doll doesn't really have brain cells to retain memories. But it's the only place she knows besides the apartment she was kept captive in. There she finds Jonathan dousing the building in gasoline.

Hate swells in her bosom busting out of her skimpy top. She storms up to him and snatches the matches out of his back pocket. She withdraws one match and tosses the other ones in his face. The little wooden sticks clatter in the pavement. Jonathan retrieves a match from the ground, and they strike them in unison. Twin flames dancing in the night.

They both hold their left arm up palms almost touching the other persons. They circle each other with their palms up and their matches held aloft.

Set that bitch on fire
Light that spark
Burn that bitch
They throw their palms back behind them
and toss their matches at the building.
Say goodbye to where we met
Both *Ignite our beginning*
It's all ashes in the end
I gave you everything
Him *still you denied me*
Attempted to murder me
You never did it for me
Her *can't make a bitch cum*
Kept me prisoner
Light that spark
Both *burn the bitch*
I gave you life
Him *you couldn't give me passion*
I'm no longer your doll
Her *you can't confine me anymore*
Light that spark

Both *burn that bitch*

The matches light the gasoline and fire swarms the building. The two of them watch it blaze, their hate for one another urging the flames on. As they watch the guy who works there pushes out the front door coughing and pulling the rest of the blowup dolls out of the fire. Rebecca moves to help him save her sisters. So pissed at Jonathan she hadn't even thought they might be in there.

The man notices Jonathan watching the building burn. "Hey! You stole Rebecca. I've been calling your ass all week. Did you do this shit?"

Jonathan flees the scene leaving Rebecca alone with him and the other blow-up dolls. The man drops a notebook while he's moving the dolls to safety and Rebecca picks it up. She notices it's the rental program for the dolls and she slides it in her panties while he's focused on the dolls. Seeing as how they're safe and so is he, Rebecca starts walking down the street the opposite direction.

She doesn't regret throwing the match on the building, but she's once more out in the cold. She has no skills so how can she even get a job? The thought of that is less scary than crawling back to Jonathan though. Fuck him.

Rebecca hears a car approaching behind her and it slows down until it's keeping pace with her. She glances over at it as the window rolls down. A big titted drag queen thrusts herself out the window,

"Rough night baby?" she asks.

"Rough life," Rebecca says.

"Your man kick you out wearing that?"

"I mean yeah, but I tried to smother him with a pillow so . . ."

The drag queen laughs. "He probably deserved it. Get in bitch."

Rebecca climbs in the back seat and comes face to face with another drag queen. A third sits behind the wheel.

The one who had leaned out the window turns around in the front and faces Rebecca. "I'm Crème de la Quim and these are my drag sisters, Tess Tickles, and Coo Chi Na Na."

"I'm Rebecca. Nice to meet you."

"You got a place to stay?" Crème de la Quim asks.

"No. I have nothing."

"You're coming home with us babe." Tess Tickles says.

"What do you want in exchange? What can I even pay you with? I have no money or job."

"We'll sort that out later. For now, you're safe with us."

Safe? Had she ever truly felt safe in Jonathan's home? Did she know what it was like to be safe? "Thank you, ladies."

The drag queens pump up the music and begin to sing and dance. Rebecca can feel the beat in her chest. It's something she's never experienced before, and she likes it. Jonathan never played music in his home. Tess Tickles gives her a nudge and a smile and Rebecca dances for the first time in her life. As she learns the words she starts to sing too. Fuck it. This is the most fun she's had since waking up in Jonathan's room. It feels like that was all a bad dream and this is the first day of her life.

The ride ends in front of a yellow bungalow with party lights wrapped around the front porch railings. The queens tumble out of the car and continue their dance up the front walk. Hesitantly Rebecca follows them. She hopes she didn't jump from the frying pan into the fire.

The three queens dance into a large room full of dresses, wigs and vanities crowded with makeup. They begin to remove their drag and

Rebecca stands in the doorway awkwardly, unsure what she should do in this strange house.

"Make yourself at home," Crème de la Quim says over her shoulder as she removes her dress. "We share everything around here."

"I don't want to appear rude but is there a place where I can sleep?" Rebecca was suddenly overcome by fatigue.

"The couch pulls out into a bed. You'll find some extra linens in the front closet."

"Thank you, girls. I really do appreciate this. I'll be out of your hair as soon as I'm able," Rebecca says.

"Don't sweat it," Coo Chi Na Na says. "You're welcome to stay with us as long as you need.

"Thank you," Rebecca says as she turns and goes to look for linens and the couch.

Despite the new environment and being surrounded by strangers, Rebecca falls asleep quickly. When she wakes up the next morning one of the queens is sitting staring at her. She can't tell which one it is because they washed all their makeup off.

She hands Rebecca a coffee. "I'm Crème De la Quim."

"Thank you for clarifying. You look so different outside of drag."

"Do you need someone to go get your clothes?"

Rebecca's eyes tear up. The drag queens had been nicer than the man that said he loved her. "All the clothes I had were skimpy like this. He wouldn't let me wear anything else."

"He made you wear that when you went out?"

"I never got to go out. He kept me at home to cook and fuck."

"Oh honey. I want to beat his ass for you. What a dick."

What a dick
What a dick
What a mighty big dick
A woman should be seen
not heard
Thinks a woman is a slave
Make him a sandwich
Suck his dick
What a dick
What a dick
What a mighty big dick
Kept me captive
Kept me ignorant
Made me lonely
Kept me plastic
What a dick
What a dick
What a mighty big dick
Stole my dignity
My virginity
Think he's a king

Said he wanted a queen
But he lied
What a dick
What a dick
What a mighty big dick

"I tried to murder him," Rebecca says.

"Good for you girl. How did the two of you meet?"

"I was a blowup doll and he wished me to life."

"Shit for real? That's insane. And he just kept you in his house like a slave?"

"Yes."

"Where this bitch live?"

"I'm not sure."

"Was he at least good in bed?"

"No." He was always concerned with his own needs. He never even tried to get her off and his foreplay was too short to even arouse her.

"He's the only man you been with as a human and he sucked in bed? Ooh girl get dressed; we're going out. Gonna get you some rebound dick and make your ex, regret everything he didn't do for you."

"I don't have any clothes."

Crème de la Quim pulls her off the couch and leads her to the drag room. "I told you we share everything."

Quim places her in front of a vanity. "I don't know how to do makeup," Rebecca says. Hell, she's never even seen herself in a mirror.

"Ooh girl, we got you. Ladies we need help in the werk room."

The other two queens enter the room and the three of them give Rebecca a makeover.

"Do I really need all of this makeup?" Rebecca asks.

"Ooh baby you got to be feeling yourself before we go out," Tess Tickles says.

"Feeling myself?"

"Didn't anyone teach you about self-love. Put your hand upon your clit. When you stroke, I stroke, we stroke."

The queens turn her chair so she can catch a glimpse of herself in the mirror. She's never looked so spectacular before and something shifts inside of her. Something new and exciting.

What's this feeling
Attraction
What's this feeling
Lust
Slip my hand inside my pants
Mmmm
Stroke
Stroke
Stroke
Mmmm
What's this feeling
Heaven
What's this feeling
Ecstasy
God I'm sexy
Touch myself
Mmmm
Stroke
Stroke

Stroke
A little bit faster now
A little bit harder now
Mmmm
My body explodes
A thousand shivers running through me
Divinity
Femininity
What's this feeling
Satisfaction
What's this feeling
Content

After she diddles her skittle, they take her to brunch and go shopping until the sun dips below the horizon and they end up at the club. "What is the purpose of this place?" Rebecca asks.

"To pick a lover by the tingling of your nethers," Coo Chi Na Na says.

"I've never picked a lover or had my nethers tingle." Other than earlier when she'd explored her own body. God that had been magnificent. Why hadn't Jonathan ever done any of that for her? Probably because he was a selfish dickhead.

The queens pick out an empty table then gesture over a waiter. They order rounds for the table then mingle with the rest of the bar. Rebecca watches them curiously. Other than Jonathan, the queens were the only other people she had ever talked to. They flit from man to man and occasionally disappear into the bathroom. Rebecca longs to be that carefree, but her time with Jonathan has made her timid.

She remains at the table slowly drinking the cocktail the queens ordered her and watch other people writhe and thrust around the dance floor. One day she hopes to be like them. Carefree. The queens dance back to her table.

"Ready to go?" Crème de la Quim asks.

Rebecca smiles at her. "Sure."

The queens dance their way to the door.

Sooo looong

And thanks for all the semen
It's been fun
Fuckin in the bathroom
It's been fun
Sooo looong
And thanks for all the semen
Turn on that firehose bitch
A sticky rain
Glistens on my skin
Sparkle sparkle bitch
Sooo looong
And thanks for all the semen
Swish and swallow
Gag me
Choke me
Hit the back of my throat
Make my eyes roll back in my head
Pussy so wet you could float
Sooo looong
And thanks for all the semen

After they get home, the drag queens undrag and fall into their beds. Rebecca pulls the notebook she hid under her pillow out. It contains the addresses of every john that had rented her. It also contained the contact information for the men who rented out her plastic sisters. They were more than sex objects and she was going to get revenge for all of them.

She falls asleep with the notebook clasped in her hands. For the second day in a row she sleeps through the night, unmolested. Now that she's met the queens and learned what attraction was, she knew she'd never had it for Jonathan.

The queens go to work the next morning with a wave and have a great day. Rebecca feels free for the first time. They don't expect dinner or sex when they return. They didn't leave her with a list of chores. They didn't put on a cooking show. There were no traditional roles in this home.

Rebecca luxuriates in a shower then heads out to find her plastic sisters. She wants to rescue them from a life of forced sex. She wanders the streets around the little shop of sex toys which is now a burned husk. She finds the owner of the shop sitting up the street with the blow-up dolls displayed around him. When his head is turned, she slips among the dolls and sits still. She feels at home among them and languishes in the feel of the sun on her skin. Before long, a man pulls up and selects one of her sisters. While he pays the shop owner, she climbs in the car next to her sister and hides. The man drives back to his home unaware she's in the car until he opens the door to carry her sister inside.

"Hell yeah, he got Rebecca back," the guy says as he removes both of them from his vehicle. "God you're heavy girl. What are they filling you with these days?"

Rebecca bites her tongue, so she doesn't respond and tip her hand too soon. He sits her in a chair in the corner of his bedroom and lays her sister Kandy on the bed. As he undresses, Rebecca spies a long thick dildo sitting on his dresser. She grabs it and comes up behind him as he climbs on top of Kandy. She slams the massive dildo into the back of his head and he tumbles off the side of the bed slamming his forehead into a bedside table with a sickening crunch.

Rebecca stands above him with the dildo raised over her head.

> *Wack that john*
> *Wack that john*
> *Put on a strap on*
> *Turn around and smack that john*
> *Fight or flight*
> *Ain't no happy endings tonight*
> *Take him from behind*
> *Hit him with this head*
> *Bang*
> *Bang*

Bang that john
Shoulda fucked with a different bitch tonight
No longer your passions hostage
Death's on the menu tonight
Wack that john
Wack that john
Turn around and smack that john
Only a fool fucks with plastic
Only a bum pays for sex
Ejaculate in crimson
Your next date is with death
Wack that john
Wack that john
Turn around and smack that john
No apologies for the life I'm livin
Sex and crime
One is divine
Freeing myself
Freeing my sisters
Fuck that pimp
Fuck that John

Wack that John

Rebecca wacks the dead man with the dildo several more times, but he doesn't move. When she steps back his ghost rises from the body.

"What the actual fuck, Rebecca?" he says as he looks from her crazed face, dildo in hand to his body lying face down on the floor with blood pooling under his head.

She shrugs. "Consent."

"Consent? She's plastic. You were plastic."

"And now you're dead. Guess you shoulda got a girlfriend instead of a doll."

"Hey, I got a sex doll, not fucking Chuckie."

"I'm sorry, would you like me to stab you with this?" Rebecca asks as she swings the dildo, and it flops in her hand.

"Don't you fucking dare."

"Fuck along to the afterlife or whatever," Rebecca says as she picks her sister up off the bed.

"Hey, I paid for her."

"Zero fucks given here," Rebecca says as she flips off his ghost and heads for the door.

"Thiiieeffff. Thiiieeff," he yells as he follows Rebecca out of his house. His little ghost throat goes raw as he screams at her but no one else hears him.

Rebecca has no idea how to drive a car, so she walks down the street carrying her blow-up sister while the dead man's ghost follows her. His cries of thief are now just screeches because his throat is raw.

"Pipe down or I'll stuff this dildo in your mouth," Rebecca says irritated.

"Consent," he garbles out.

Rebecca rolls her eyes and keeps walking. She ends up back by the burnt husk of the little shop of sex toys. The owner, Marty is sitting on the sidewalk drinking a beer, with the sex dolls around him on the pavement.

"Look at us now, girls," he says.

"You gonna murder him too?" the ghost croaks.

"I don't know. Maybe." For now, she wants him alive so he can keep bringing the men to her. She was going to Wack every last John that had purchased time with her and her sisters.

She ducks into the unsafe little shop of sex toys and roots among the burnt toys. She kicks aside a scorched box and finds a mostly undamaged strap on. She attaches it and hides it in her pants. She learned how to tuck from her new drag friends.

Rebecca tucks her sister into a corner. "I'll be back for you," she tells the doll before going back outside. Marty is negotiating with another john, so she slips unseen into the man's car.

She hears Marty yell "if my prices don't suit you then drive into the next county and get a real prostitute."

The man gets back in the car and slams the door. The car pulls away from the curb and into traffic before the man notices Rebecca in the back seat via the mirror.

"Oh hello," he says. "Where did you come from?"

Rebecca remains silent.

"Alright, keep your secrets."

During the drive he keeps looking in the rearview mirror to make sure he didn't dream her sitting back there. Next to her is the ghost of the first john shaking his head. Of course, this new guy can't see the dead, so he has no idea what awaits him when he gets her home.

He carries her into his two-story home and takes her to the upstairs bedroom where he tosses her unceremoniously on the bed. He steps up on the bed and towers over her with a smile. Rebecca yanks her pants down and her strap on pops out erect. The man throws his head back and laughs then pulls his pants down. Instead of a penis he's got a scarred-up area. He licks the tips of his fingers on both hands then rubs them down his scarred flesh while biting his lip.

"What the hell?" she says, her eyes growing wide.

He grabs a strap on from the bedside table, puts it on, and swings his hips a little so it wiggles. Rebecca surges to her feet and their strap-ons collide in the weirdest fucking sword fight ever. She pushes him off the bed and jumps down.

Let's have a dick fight
I wana have dick fight
Thrust
Parry
Thrust
Parry
I'll wack you with my johnson
Take it like a man
Take it like a man
I'll wack you with my johnson
Take it like a man

Bend over
Rebecca *I'll show you where this goes*
Get on your knees
Him *I'll show you where this goes*
Both *Mine's bigger*
Mine's longer
Catch me with this big dick energy
Catch me with my trousers down
Catch me as a top
I'll wack you with my johnson
Take it like a man
Take it like a man
I'll wack you with my johnson
Take it like a man

Rebecca continues her strap on attack and forces the man backward out of the bedroom and to the top of the stairs where he loses his footing and falls down the stairs backward. He tumbles ass over legs and lands at the bottom with his neck bent at an odd angle. His ghost steps out of his body.

"God damnit, not another one," Rebecca says.

"I tried to warn you," the first ghost says. "I'm Cliff by the way."

"Ian," the second ghost says. "What the hell's her deal?"

"Consent," Cliff says.

"She was laying right there. That's consent."

"I'm saying. She wanted me to get consent from a blowup doll."

"This bitch," Ian says.

Jonathan sits in his car on the street of sin one town over. He's decided since wishing his dream girl to life didn't work in his favor, he's going to build the perfect woman. A Frankenhooker if you will.

Killing hookers
Look at those legs
Check out those breasts
Oh god that sternum

Show me those ankles
Killing hookers
Take the best parts
Throw away the scraps
Collect those pieces
Rebuild that bitch
Look at that ass
Check out those clavicles
Oh god those lips
Show me some shoulder
Take and make a lover
Reduce, recycle, reuse
Destruct
Reconstruct
Killing hookers
Look at that nose
Check out that hair
Oh god those legs
Show me those eyes
Killing hookers

Jonathan invites several hookers into his car and took them to his home where he introduces them to an ax he got at the local hardware store.

Rebecca walks her tired ass back to the drag queen's home. She's followed by the ghosts of all the men she killed that day. No matter what she tries they continue to follow her. They all believe they were murdered unjustly, but they cannot sway her in her mission to kill all the men who took advantage of her and her sisters.

The ghosts follow her into the drag house and Rebecca finds the queen's are back from their jobs. Coo Chi Na Na watches Rebecca and her unwanted stalkers enter the home.

"Who the hell are all those ghosts?" Coo Chi Na Na asks.

"Men I killed for not asking my blowup sisters consent before having sex with them."

"What are they doing here?"

"They think they need to punish me for their murders. I think they're just pissed they all got murdered with a strap on."

"I think I can help. Girls get my crystal ball!" Coo Chi Na Na yells.

Rebecca sits on her bed while the queens get dressed in their medium outfits. She tries not to laugh at the ghosts because they're all wearing what they died in and it's not flattering. The queens enter the room with a round table, four chairs, and a crystal ball. They set the items up then beckon Rebecca to join them around the table. Coo Chi Na Na urges them to all hold hands then she tips her head back as far as she can.

Come one come all
You wretched souls
Follow my voice and I'll usher you on
Your time is passed
Enter your afterlife
Haunting is for fools

You all look like tools and you act like ghouls
The ghosts *No crime in sowing*

our oats

No crime in passion

We were wrongfully murdered

We're not leaving without her

Coo Chi Na Na waves her hands over the crystal ball, and it glows.

Open the portal

Receive these souls

The ghosts *we're not leaving*

can't make us go

we call on Hekate

we call on Lilih

make these sinners pay

so come one come all

you wretched souls

enter the light

Red glows from the crystal ball and they shrink until they are eyes on a smoky dog-like creature. It snarls then leaps out of the crystal ball and chases the ghosts right out the front door.

Coo Chi Na Na rubs her hands together in a gesture that says she's done with that situation. "Now, no more killing."

"Listen mama, these men were horrible, and they've been trading me and my sisters around for their pleasure. They deserve what they get."

Jonathan sews the last piece of body to his Frankenhooker and marvels over the masterpiece he has created.

Perfect by design
Flawless
Creature of love
Rise darling rise
Come alive
Rise darling rise
Complete me
Keep me
Embrace us

Rise darling rise
Come alive
Rise darling rise
Built for love
Constructed by beauty
Oh impeccable angel
With your first breath
You catch my scent
My imprint on you
Rise darling rise
Come alive
Rise darling rise
With a spark
I give you life
Take my hand
Be my wife
Rise darling rise

Jonathan throws the switch and electricity pulses through her body. He lets it run for two minutes before he shuts it off and looks at the body he assembled. Her fingers start to twitch and then her legs begin jerking. He watches her body convulse almost like she's seizing and then she sits up abruptly.

Jonathan gingerly touches her shoulder, and she turns to look at him. He brushes her hair behind her ear. "I am Jonathan, your husband. Do you know this word husband?"

The Frankenhooker screams until her throat bleeds, and it turns to a gargle. Jonathan stands next to her with his fingers in his ears. It would be just his luck that both of his women screamed bloody murder when they woke up next to him.

"Are you done?" he yells.

She closes her mouth and stares at him. Jonathan removes his fingers. "I'm going to call you Francine."

Francine vomits down her front. Jonathan gags but helps her off the table.

"Let's get you into a shower. Then maybe take a walk so you can get the hang of life and your parts."

Jonathan helps Francine to the shower then dresses her in a tiny dress and flats. He takes her hand and leads her out onto the sidewalk. So far, she's quiet and he hopes she's not brain dead from the surgery. Her hand is limp in his and he clutches it tighter. He doesn't mean for it too, but his steps lead them past the burnt-up sex shop. Unbidden, thoughts of Rebecca surface and almost like his thoughts conjure her, Rebecca steps out of the burnt husk of the store.

Rebecca sees them and stops, her eyes riveted to Francine. Jonathan feels Francine stop and he glances over to see her just as magnetized to Rebecca.

"No no no," Jonathan says.

Rebecca and Francine

I've got tingles
In my nethers
What is this feeling
Oh fuck, I'm horny
My insides quiver
And my panties drip
Bink bink
Nipples taut
Oh fuck, I'm horny
Fatal attraction
Please tell me you feel it too
Oh god, just touch me
La la la lick me
Fa fa fa fuck me
Oh fuck, I'm horny
Shred my clothes
Claw me like an animal

Jonathan tugs Francine's hand and she pulls toward Rebecca. Rebecca closes the distance between her and Francine and smashes her lips into hers. Their tongues embrace inside their joined mouths.

"Oh, what the fuck," Jonathan yells and stamps his foot.

Rebecca pulls out of the kiss and wraps her arm around Francine. "She's mine bro."

"I fucking made her," Jonathan says.

Rebecca pulls out the dildo she killed the first john with and sticks it in Jonathan's face. "Fuck off."

Jonathan holds up his hands and backs up a step.

"Work on yourself before you find a new woman. Or I'll be back to use this," Rebecca says.

Rebecca and Francine throw up some peace signs and wander down the street arm in arm content to see where this horniness goes.

Both *Everybody get*
    Everybody get
    Everybody get freak nasty
    Everybody fuck

Everybody fuck
Everybody fuck freak nasty
We're buckin
And fuckin
A little bit naughty
A lotta nasty

Rebecca *bite me*
                    Spank me
                    Pull my hair

Francine *I like whips*
                    I like chains
                    Tie me up
                    Strip me down

Rebecca *I'll be your prancing pony*
                    I'll be your slave

Francine *Be my deviant*
                    Be my master
                    Real freaky
                    Real naughty
                    Real freaky
                    Real naughty

Everybody get
Everybody get
Everybody get freak nasty
Everybody fuck
Everybody fuck
Everybody fuck freak nasty
ravish me
Dominate me
Choke me
Make me filthy
I'll be passions hostage
We'll be passions hostage

Gargoyle sex and the power of Christ

I push my way through the writhing bodies on the dance floor of club Baron, the hottest nightclub in the city. The bass of the current song vibrating in my chest as I move toward the bar. Bodies writhe around me as people grind against each other. I am in my happy place, the smell of sex and sweat permeating the air and mixing with the smell of the fog machines. The twin owners, Logan and Lathan lean on the bar. Both wear identical dark grey suits with blood red ties. Lathan holds a drink in his hand watching the crowd while Logan flirts with a woman sitting at the bar. I slide between the twins and lean my elbows on the bar motioning to the bartender. He slides me my usual. I come here more than I should, but the vibe of raw sex appeals to me. I turn and take Logan by the arm moving his attention away from the woman at the bar.

"I need you."

The woman looks at me with a sneer. "We were talking."

Logan looks between us as Lathan chuckles.

"And now you're done," I say.

"Business or pleasure?" Logan asks.

"Business."

"I was going to ask if you were trying to make me jealous," Lathan says. "But since you said business, I'm glad you chose him."

"Are you seriously going to pick her over me?" the girl asks Logan.

"She needs me," Logan says.

The girl throws her drink in Logan's face then stomps into the crowd of people. Lathan laughs as Logan wipes himself off with a towel the bartender hands him.

"I hope you're happy Kitra," Logan says to me, tossing the towel on the bar.

I grab his shirt front and pull him after me. "Quit whining, you're still getting laid."

"But did you see her legs?"

"Those were some nice legs." I'm not picky when it comes to my lovers. Having almost died once I like to enjoy the pleasures of life. If you're breathing, you're pretty much fair game.

"They would have looked great in my collection."

I had seen Logan's collection. It was nice. Logan and Lathan were both gargoyles and with that came an unfortunate side effect. Their semen turned people to stone. Logan celebrated this fact and kept some of his favorite lovers as statues in his bedroom. And until the invention of condoms neither of the gargoyles ever got to finish. Their semen is why I needed them. It would turn any creature to stone, not just humans. The only one's immune were other gargoyles. Unlike when I asked him for pleasure, Logan did not lead me to his bedroom filled with Kama sutra statues that used to be his lovers. When I say business, he takes me to his office that overlooks the night club. He unbuckles his pants and leaned back against his desk. He might be willing, but he was going to make me work for it, especially since I made him miss out on those legs. I take a moment to admire him like that, pants undone leaning against his desk.

"What's the job?" Logan asks.

"Saving a human junkie from a vampire coven. Her parents want her back."

"There are easier ways to get rid of vampires."

There were. But this job was personal. The coven that had her used to have me. They'd very nearly killed me on a cleansing night. "I also have a client looking for vampire statues." I make my living from creature art. Saving humans from the things that go bump in the night pays jack shit.

Slowly I cross the room and slip my hand inside his pants. Despite being a gargoyle, his flesh is warm and soft like a human's until I stroke him to stiffness. While he puts on a condom I move to my knees before him.

The first time I'd met him he'd tried not to use a condom and I'd tried to kill him. He'd eventually saw I was not statue worthy and I'd seen not all monsters are bad.

I take him into my mouth and begin to tease him with my tongue. Logan twists his hand in my hair and thrusts against my mouth. His tip slams into the back of my throat and I pull back just enough to tease it with my tongue. He thrusts several more times before pulling me off by my hair.

"My turn," he says.

Logan scoops me up and places me on the desk licking his way down my neck to the crease between my breasts. I don't try to stop him as little shivers course through me. He peels my shirt off over my head and unsnaps my bra.

"I said business," I say as his hand skims up my thigh and under my short skirt. I'm not mad. He's good at what he does. And I'm addicted to pleasures of the flesh.

"I like to mix business with pleasure."

His hand encounters no resistance since I don't wear panties. Logan's fingers stroke me until I'm wet while his tongue makes circles around my nipples. He positions himself between my legs and I moan as he slides inside me. I wrap my legs around his waist as he thrusts, and he grips my hips to thrust faster. I lift my hips and meet each of his thrusts, pushing him deeper. My head tips back and I watch people on the dance floor upside down through the window in his office. Some of them are fucking while they dance, and it makes me wetter. I watch them as he thrusts inside me until I cum. He gives one final thrust before he cums as well and eases down onto me for a minute while we both breathe heavy.

"Pleasure doing business with you," I say as he withdraws and removes his condom.

Logan pours the contents of his condom into a container and hands it to me. It isn't the first time he's given me it and it won't be the last. I fix my skirt before tucking the container in my pocket and pull on my shirt. "Thank you."

"Be careful out there," Logan says as I head out of his office. I go back down to the bar where Lathan is watching my drink.

"I feel cheated," Lathan says. "You said it was business but looks like you had pleasure."

I take a sip from my drink and turn to look at him. "I'm up for some more pleasure if you're still willing."

Lathan has never liked the business of me using their semen to turn creatures to stone. That's why our relations are strictly for pleasure, whereas Logan had no qualms about what I do with his semen. Lathan tips my chin up and kisses me passionately.

"I don't think you have time for that."

I knew he was right. Of the two Lathan is more level-headed. He was generally thinking of others unlike myself and Logan. I needed to go get the girl from the vampires, not keep fucking. But god, I could. Lathan was even more thorough in his love making than Logan. As far as I knew he only had one stone person. And he kept her behind a set of curtains. I think he may have actually been in love with her. And I'd only seen her because I'd snuck a peek when he was in the bathroom.

"Raincheck." I drink the rest of my drink and head out of the club.

A chilly misty rain sprays the city as I go home to get my gear. My tiny one-bedroom apartment is in the attic of an abandoned building. Because of the work I do I can't afford to have a real address. Monsters are vindictive when you hurt or kill one of them and over the years, I've done plenty of that. But I figure it's fair since the vamps almost did me in. Inside my gear kit I throw the usual, wooden stakes, holy water, and crucifixes. Those items are only a last-ditch effort. I don't want to kill the vampires, only encase them in stone so I can sell them as statues. When I'm not out fucking with monsters, I'm selling statues of them to the art community. A career I'd sort of stumbled into after meeting Logan and Lathan one night. Up until that point I'd been hunting monsters for cash. No one else wanted the job and someone had to hold them responsible for the chaos they created. Sure, there were safer jobs like body clean up for the different families who ran the city, but there was no adrenaline in that.

When I'm done filling my backpack with objects of destruction, I take two spray bottles, pour half the semen into one and half into the other, then add water and give them a good shake to mix. Each of those I affix to the outside of my bag then throw it on and walk to the vampire coven that has the girl. I'd never had the resources to move far from them but hey they thought I was dead and never came looking for me. And even if I pass one on the street, they don't seem to recognize me.

Vampires like to take young people and keep them for food. They slowly drink from them until one day they drink too much and kill them. Most of the humans are volunteers who get high on the idea of vampires. Little nerds who were in way over their heads. No judgement, I'd been one. Vampires were glorified in movies. Every dumb girl who thought she needed them to be special ended up as food. The rest were addicted to a drug the vampires had they called Christ's blood. One taste was enough to make the humans do anything the vampires wanted. I'd been addicted once too. When I woke up to what was happening to me and tried to leave, they'd gotten me hooked on it so I couldn't.

The coven house sits downtown and was the only building not falling apart for at least three blocks. The building itself had once been a courthouse. Because the vampires can't risk stray light coming in the streetlights surrounding the building have been busted out and the glass crunches under my feet as I approach. I know the two guards at the front door can smell me, but they aren't threatened by a human and let me get close. That's their mistake. I spray both of them and they turn to stone on either side of the door. With no fangs out they wouldn't be worth much.

I enter and the tang of blood hits me in the face. It's feeding time. Hazy memories from my own time as a bleeder swirls in my head and I'm nearly undone. I let my memories guide me to the dining room. Naked bodies cover the long dining table and the vampires are biting any piece of flesh they can get their fangs in. Bile surges into my throat. They only eat like this when they're done with this crop and are ready for something new. All of these people are going to die tonight. So, overcome by their bloodlust the vampires don't notice me standing in the doorway. I could easily dispatch all of them like that, but I need them fangs bared for good statues. I whistle and their keen hearing helps them hear over their slurping. One by one they turn to look at me and bare their blood red dripping fangs with a hiss. I smile.

"Now that I've got your attention."

They lung at me and I begin spraying them. A few of the young ones try to run before they're turned to stone, the older ones try to attack but my sprays are too quick, and the semen reacts to their skin even faster confining them to stone. When they are all solid, I put the bottles down and approach the table. One by one I check the bodies for pulses, hoping for one, but it's too late. The only good thing is I don't see the girl I've been sent to find among the bodies. At least I don't have to tell her mother I was too late. I take a minute of silence to pay respect to the bodies on the table. I had been one of them once. I shouldn't be here, but I was. I send a quick text to my cleaner to come get the statues and then go room by room, level by level looking for the girl, but don't find her.

The last place to look is behind a steel door I vaguely remember goes to the sublevels. A place food was never allowed to go. I ease the heavy door open and am surprised it opens silently. A set of stone steps descend into darkness. I remove a flashlight from my bag and one of the spray bottles. Holding them in front of me I slowly make my way down the steps into the dark. My flashlight barely illuminates the thick blackness. When I reach the bottom of the stairs I feel around for a light switch. Light illuminates a circular room with no other doors or windows. A male body lays naked on a slab in the middle of the room. He has an IV attached to him and it appears to be removing blood from him. A tall table stands next to the slab with a bottle of wine and a box of communion crackers on it. I approach and notice his eyes are closed. His dark hair is greasy and plastered against a pale forehead. I lift his lips and check for fangs before putting my spray bottle away. I can't just leave him, so I unstrap him from the table and the device. His eyes remain closed and I shake him a little. Drearily his eyes open then drop close.

"Yo, dude. Come on." I shake him again and his eyes open for longer.

"Ffffeed me," he says.

I crinkle my nose at the communion crackers and wine, but I stick one in his mouth then pour wine in after it. This seems to revive him somewhat and he's able to help me get him into an upright position. He eats some more wafers and takes the wine bottle from my hand then pours a large gulp in his mouth and swallows as some spills out the sides and coats his skin. When he puts the bottle down, I help him get off the table. He reaches back and grabs the bottle again, so I grab the box of wafers and we start toward the stairs with him leaning against me. Slowly we go up with one of his arms draped across my shoulders and he's drinking wine with the other hand. He looks like he can't weigh much but he's starting to slow me down. With each swig his steps became steadier. He is almost moving on his own when we get to the top of the stairs. He slowly looks around as I half drag him to the front door. Tucking the cracker box under my other arm, I open the door and come face to face with a ball of snakes. Several strike me in the face and I stumble back and fall, hitting my head on the doorframe. I drop to my knees, my hand sliding off of the man. I look up into the face of a gorgeous woman wearing sunglasses. Snakes writhe around her head like hair. She stomps me in the face and the world goes dark.

I wake on a lumpy couch, sun glinting through a broken blind into my face. I can hear the sizzle of something frying and hear the muted notes of singing mixed with hissing. With a groan I sit up and look around. The room I'm in is furnished with items that are either second hand or very old. The tv is at least ten years old and the recliner is faded and ripped. The couch I'm on looks even older and has mysterious stains on it. Disgusted I move to my feet and go toward the sounds and smells of frying bacon.

"Sorry about last night. Hopefully the bacon makes up for it, or are you vegan?" The smell of the bacon pulls me forward and my stomach grumbles. The woman stands at the stove, a mess of snakes writhing around her head. Some of them turn and hiss at me as I approach. "Pay them no mind, they're cranky," she says without turning.

"Are they poisonous?" I ask remembering their bites and touch my face.

"Only mildly toxic unless you're a man."

I wonder if that's what happened to the guy, I brought out of the vamp coven, but before I can ask there is a knock on her door.

"Can you get that please?" she asks.

I find the request weird considering she basically kidnapped me, but I turn to oblige her. On the way to the door I pass back through the living room where I woke up and notice a shrine with a stone baby sitting on it wrapped in a blanket. Before I can look closer the knock comes again. I open the door and find two men dressed in suits.

"Have you met our lord and savior?" one of them asks.

The woman yells from the kitchen. "Oh yes honey, he's asleep in the back bedroom."

The men look startled. "Um . . . huh?"

I'm just as confused as them and wondering if she means she turned him to stone and he's eternally sleeping. I can't really frown on her for doing that when I've turned numerous creatures to stone.

"I think we're good," I say. "Thanks though." I shut the door and go look closer at the shrine. There are pictures of the woman with a rounded stomach and sonograph pictures. The sight makes me sad for her.

"Breakfast," the woman calls.

Reluctantly I pull myself from the shrine and go in the kitchen. She sets three places with plates full of bacon, hash browns, and scrambled eggs. I sit in front of one. "Where's the guy from last night?"

"He's sleeping in the back bedroom. I just said that," she says.

I slowly eat while she devours her plate with her mouth and snakes. We eat in silence and no one sits at the third plate.

"Why am I here?" I ask.

"Well I couldn't just leave you there. Especially since I paid you to be there. That's a bad investment."

My fork clatters to my plate. "You what?"

"Surprise, the girl you were looking for was never there. I was after the man you carried out."

"Then why didn't you just hire me to get him out?"

"I thought you'd leave once you found out she wasn't dinner," the woman says with a shrug.

"What's he to you?" I ask.

"Salvation."

I had been around long enough to know salvation did not exist. No one came to save you. Not in this city. Except for the occasional hum from the snakes attached to her head the rest of breakfast was silent. When we're done, I help her clear the table, but she leaves the full plate

"Come on, he's back here," she says leading me down a hall. He is laying on the bed with a blanket draped over him. He's not stone which means he was neither bitten nor did she look at him. His breath rises and falls, but his eyes remain closed.

"You gonna wake him?" I ask. I'm unsure how a man can be salvation, but then I'd never followed gender roles.

"No, I need him at full strength."

"For what?"

"The resurrection," she says.

"He's just a dude." I'm almost sick, because here is this uber powerful woman and she's pining for this dude that up until the night before had been a snack for a den of vamps.

"No, he's Christ the Christian lord."

"What?" I couldn't believe the man I'd pulled from that basement was Jesus Christ, but it kind of makes sense. The vamps kept their feeders there by giving them something they called the blood of Christ. I'd been addicted to it once myself. The high had been surreal and coming off of it had been hell.

The woman motions me to follow her and we go back to the living room. She stands in front of the shrine, her back to me and starts whispering to the stone. "It won't be long now," she whispers.

I sit on the lumpy couch and watch her warily. I've seen a lot of beings turned into stone. Never have I seen one saved.

"I'm sure you've figured out who I am," she says.

"A gorgon."

"The gorgon. Medusa."

"No shit? Huge fan. What's with the baby?" I ask. I'd never heard a legend of Medusa stating she had a baby.

"It's hers," a male voice says.

We both turn and I see the guy I saved standing in the doorway with the blanket wrapped around his waist.

"She wants me to save him," he says.

"Please Jesus," she says, "he's innocent."

Jesus approaches the shrine and pricks his thumb. He makes the sign of the cross on the baby's forehead with his blood. The stone recedes and the baby starts crying. The sound is atrocious, but I mean I'm happy for her if this is what she wants.

The woman has tears in her eyes as she approaches. "Momma's here," she says as she picks the baby up and holds him to her breast. "Thank you," she mumbles as she leaves the room with the baby.

Jesus sinks into the tattered recliner like he's exhausted and closes his eyes.

"You really Jesus?" I ask. Not because I doubt the existence of the guy. Not after all the creatures and gods I have seen in this city. But what were the odds Jesus was being farmed in a vamp den.

"In the flesh. It's the second coming baby." His tone makes it sound like a joke, but he doesn't smile, and the expression seems almost ominous.

"Isn't that your time to shine or whatever? Shouldn't you be happy?"

"The second coming was never designed to be a happy affair. Shit'll get real now."

"Jesus Christ why don't you come with a warning?"

"Yes."

"No not you, like that, fuck. Like what the hell, I thought you were human." Had I known saving him would set about the second coming I might have left him. Fuck, I need to clear my head and sex is a great way to do that. I need Lathan. I get up and head for the door.

"Where you going?" Jesus asks.

"To get some dick," I say. To my shock the good lord's face doesn't turn red. For dramatic flair I want to slam the door behind me, but I'm cognizant of the newborn and ease the door closed. I'm not a complete bitch.

I walk into club Baron even though its not open yet. I know I'll find both Lathan and Logan inside. They never seem to sleep. Unlike other times there is a woman standing between the two. She has short straight raven black hair and blood red lips that smile at my approach.

"Rough night?" Logan asks.

"Rough enough," I say. "Lathan you got a minute?"

Lathan grabs at his heart. "A minute? I'm hurt."

The woman's head tips as her reptilian eyes look me up and down. "I've got a minute to spare."

Instantly lust coils low in my belly and I want her. I hadn't paid her much attention when I walked in but now that I'm really looking at her, she's the most beautiful person I have ever seen.

"Kitra meet Lucy Feral," Logan says.

Her snake like eyes look deep into mine and a forked tongue flicks out of her mouth. "I can smell your lust," she says.

A small smile flits across my lips. I like her. "But can you taste it?" God what I wouldn't give for her to taste it.

Lucy smiles again before her tongue flicks out and slides up under my skirt. "I can."

"Never mind Lathan, I'm curious what a minute with her is like," I say.

"We can all take a minute," Lathan says as he moves behind me.

He slides my shirt over my head, and she flicks my nipples with her forked tongue. Somebody's hands pull my skirt off and soon I'm naked and the other three are touching and licking my body. They lay me across the bar and one of them sucks my nipples while she flicks her forked tongue across my clit. I moan as a mouth covers mine. We become a writhing mass of hands and tongues and moans before I feel something slip inside of me and rock against me. This situation is all about my pleasure and they are nailing it. Whoever is inside me withdraws and I feel her forked tongue flick inside of me and taste. My god does she taste. My body spasms as I come from the flicks of her tongue. She cleans me with her tongue, and they dress me in my clothes.

I feel better after their intense treatment of my body and I walk behind the bar to make a drink.

"Where is Jesus?" Lucy asks.

"Left him at Medusa's joint. How'd you know he's Jesus?" I ask.

She smiles as she reapplies her lipstick. "I'm Lucifer baby. And unfortunately, the son of man has a role to fill." Lucy air kisses at me and walks out of the bar.

"What the hell did you get yourself into Kitra?" Logan asks.

I shrug. "No more than usual."

"Lucifer seems to think you started the apocalypse."

I shrug again. "Someone had to I guess."

"You don't feel bad about it?" Lathan asks.

"Eh, not really. I am curious what she's going to do with Jesus, so if you'll excuse me." I chase after Lucy, and not just because she's smoking hot and good at oral. I genuinely want to see what Jesus role in this apocalypse scenario is. I hadn't noticed before but she's wearing stilettos and a skintight black pinstripe suit. She's marching down the sidewalk and I run to catch up.

"You really should get off the street," she says. "My pet will be released tonight."

"Which one?"

"The destroying angel. You're not a first born, are you?"

"Only child."

"Oh shit. Better ask the lamb for some of his blood to put on your door."

"What?"

"Never heard of the Passover?" she asks.

"Nope, not the most religious."

"I'll make sure he gives you some of his blood. I'm interested to see what you think of what's coming next."

I was interested too. How much more fucked up could a city full of monsters become. Although I was a little sad, I would never get to spend the cash from selling those vampire statues. What good would money be when the world went to shit. And if Lucy was to be believed, it was starting when the sun went down.

"How did you end up with the name Lucy Feral?" I ask as we continue to Medusa's house.

"I got tired of everyone shitting their pants when I introduced myself as Lucifer."

I laugh. "I'm sure that smells awful."

"Ugh you've no idea. God has killed more people than me, but I'm the terrifying one."

We continue our amicable chat while we walk to Medusa's. When we get there, Lucy knocks which surprises me. I'm somewhat shocked she has manners and didn't walk right in. Medusa answers the door wearing sunglasses and holding her baby. She seems happy now that her child is once more flesh.

"Where's Jesus?" Lucy asks.

"I don't know. He left."

Lucy huffs. "He knows he has a role to play."

"He knows the vamp den, maybe he went there," I say.

"We can hope," Lucy says turning from the door then turns back toward Medusa. "If he didn't wipe his blood on your door, then I'd get out of town before the sun goes down. The angel of destruction is coming."

I lead Lucy toward the vampire den. "Why didn't god save Jesus from the vampires? Did he not know where he was?"

"He knew exactly where he was, but they had an arrangement. Jesus would feed the vamps so they weren't feeding on humans and if he ever was rescued from them then it would be considered the second coming. Neither of them wants this. Hell, I don't either. But, so let it be written, so let it be done."

"Where the hell was that written. I'm no religious scholar, but I don't recall ever hearing about Jesus being a blood whore to the vampires."

"They weren't advertising. But the vamps got cocky. That's how Medusa knew where to find Jesus to save her child."

"Did Medusa know what would happen by taking Jesus from the vamps?" I ask. She seemed like a nice person; I couldn't believe she'd knowingly condemn the world.

"If you had any children, you'd get it," Lucy says.

"Do you have children?" She doesn't seem the mothering type, but she's had centuries to be one.

"Kind of. Like the creature I'm releasing tonight, I consider it my child."

"Can I see it?" I'll admit I'm morbidly curious what Lucifer considers a child.

"Trust me, you don't want to. It's designed for one thing."

We continue toward the vamp den. Even if Christ isn't there, I'm hoping some of his blood is there for me to use on a few doorways. I don't care about the general public, but I do have a few firstborn friends in this city. And I think its really cool that Lucy warned Medusa since her son is probably her first born. The street is quiet, and I think maybe the city has felt what's coming, and part of me wants to be sick because I started it. If I had died in the vamp den, Christ would have never been released. Although I'm confused why Medusa needed me when she can also turn people to stone.

The vamp den is empty when we arrive, and I walk straight down to the dungeon not bothering to see where Lucy goes. Just like I hope I find the contraption that had been taking Christ's blood from him. I remove the bag of blood and go back upstairs. Lucy is standing in the dining room and Jesus is nowhere around.

"We can save a few," I say as I show her the bag of blood.

"Save who you want. At sundown I let my child free. The angel of destruction walks free again." With that Lucy disappears in a column of fire.

I got back to Medusa's and put blood around her doorway then I go to the club and put blood around their doors. After that I use the last of the blood for my own door. There is some blood left and I put it in my fridge. You never know when you might need the blood of Christ.

As the sun disappears, I stare out my window. The sunset is blood red. Lucy appears on my doorstep with a cage in her hand. There is something smoky inside. Something about it gives me the creeps. As the last rays of the sun disappears Lucy opens the cage. The smoke cloud explodes from it and shoots down the street.

I watch the angel of destruction grow and spread out like a fog over the city. Unsuspecting people walk through it. Some are unfazed, the others; the firstborns are seized by it. Their bodies contort and turn into hideous creatures. The creatures then start attacking people and ripping them to shreds. Tonight, the streets run red with blood. I'm watching paralyzed. I can't help them, and I'm not sure I even want to. No guilt fills me at what I started, and I wonder if I'm as bad as the monsters that held me captive for food. I know I should go to bed and try to get some rest because who knows what tomorrow will bring, but part of me has a morbid curiosity to see how bad tonight gets. I suppose it's not long before the rioting and looting start, so I pour a drink and make a bag of popcorn, then I pull the comfiest chair I have over to the window and just watch. Its amazing how crazy the average human can get in a situation like this. Night turns to the pink of dawn and some of the screams die out. The monsters seem to retreat into empty buildings and avoid the light. Lucy Feral knocks on my front door and I open it, but she remains outside.

She gestures where I spread the lord's blood. "Kinda need an invite to pass something protected by his blood."

"Oh, so like a vampire?"

Lucy laughs. "Kinda yeah."

"If I let you in does that mean anything can come past the blood?" I don't need any other monsters waltzing in here.

"Nope, just me. Kind of a one and done thing."

"Okay, you can come in," I say stepping aside.

Lucy Feral smirks at my chair and snack set up. "You should have gotten some sleep."

"It was interesting to watch. And I was slightly worried the blood wouldn't stop the monsters."

"You're right it wouldn't have. It only works on denizens of evil like myself and the Angel of destruction."

"What happens next?" I ask. I'm not up to speed on my biblical apocalypses.

"I reign for seven years. Things are going to get bad."

"Yeah, that's what Jesus said."

"I'd like to offer you a proposition. I like to have fun; you like to have fun. And this way I can make sure you stay safe through the next seven years."

"What exactly are you asking?" I ask.

"Be my sex slave."

"Can I still fuck other . . . beings." It had been awhile since I'd fucked a human, but I very much enjoyed my entanglements with the gargoyle twins.

"As long as it's inside my palace."

I shrug. "What the hell."

Plagues and weather phenomena rock the globe for the first year of Lucy's reign. By the second one things have mostly evened out. Sure, there are gangs roving the cities, but most of the monsters have either died or moved on from the city we're in. At least that's the rumor I hear. As Lucy Feral's favored pet I don't see a lot but the ceiling because of all the orgies.

With her I don't have to worry about where my next meal or orgasm comes from. Sure, the rest of the human race hates me, but I'm being forked every night by Lucy Feral's serpent tongue and no ones feeding off of me except the sex demons and they ask first. It's not like it was with the vampires. I'm not on Christ's blood to feel good and I'm mutually respected. I say to myself as I wear a gold chain around my neck that's attached to Lucy's throne. Don't get me wrong, I've enjoyed being her plaything. I've enjoyed not fighting the rest of the world for scraps for once in my life. But I'm also kind of bored. And I know it's not safe out there with the rest of the humans who despise me for being in Lucifer's bed, but a part of me wants to see what the world has turned into. Lucy only lets me see glimpses. Like she's afraid if she takes my focus off of her sex parties that I'll grow to hate her. Maybe I should. The rest of the world sure does, but they were all doomed anyway. We all were.

Lucy's forked tongue flicks across my breasts and I'm pulled out of my thoughts in time to hear her say "They think I'm weak. That my preference for a human has made me so. Otherwise I never would have baby."

My mind spins and I manage to mutter 'huh' as a liquid splashes across me. The neck chain falls at my feet and I feel stone start to set into my bones. I pull the vial of leftover Christ's blood from inside my tiny top and drink it. I knew one day I'd need it.

Lucy screams. "God damnit. I was doing this for your own good. They would see you hadn't made me weak and you'd be safe in your stone shell for the next six years."

I'm not sure what I've done to myself as the blood makes my head spin and a high start to settle behind my eyes. But I feel the stone feeling begin to recede and I sprint from the throne room. Lucy doesn't even bother to follow me, the bitch. How could she do this to me? All she had to do was tell me to get out. Jesus, who decides to turn someone to stone all of a sudden. And then I remember. Logan would. And I know for a fact it was his semen she threw on me. Betrayed by two lovers at once. Hot tears pour down my cheeks. Sure, I never expected forever from either of them. And I'd never wanted it, but what the fuck did I do to either to be encased in stone. God that was my worst fear. Being stuck there unable to move or talk but unable to look away from what happened around you. And these two mother fuckers that I had trusted had tried to do that to me for no god damned reason. I race past my room not bothering to stop for clothes. All of them fucking look like what I got on. An invitation to fuck. I am the sex symbol of the fucking apocalypse and I dress as such. I run out of the palace, unguarded because why would Lucifer need guards. And I don't stop running until I make it back to the building, I had been living in prior to the shit hole I had helped make the world. Christ's dried blood is still crusted to the door frame that is swollen and trying to rot, but his blood keeps it intact. None of my shit has really been looted because it's shit as well.

My feet are cracked and bleeding from running barefoot through the city and I sit down to wrap them. The high of Jesus blood is starting to wane a little and I desperately want more. The stuff is highly addictive, just ask the Christians. I was addicted once before, and I refuse to go back. Once my feet are bandaged, I look in my tiny closet and find one outfit left. I guess my pink hail Satan t-shirt made the rest of the world uncomfortable since she is now lord of the land. I inwardly groan as I put it on. Nothing like breaking up with Lucifer and then having to wear a hail Satan t-shirt. Fuck my life. And now I'm going to fuck hers.

Lucy thinks she gets to rule the world for the next six years, because it was prophesied and blah blah blah. Fuck the prophets. And fuck that bitch. I'm going to prove them all wrong. And Christ above is going to help me. Once I find him that is. No one has seen the good lord since he left Medusa's house. And she'd told me and Lucy that she didn't know where he went, but maybe that had changed. Couldn't hurt to ask and see if she had a cooler shirt. One that didn't make me wana rage vomit every time I thought about it.

Now that I'm dressed, and my feet are bandaged there is nothing holding me back. I leave my place once again and head across town to where Medusa used to live. I hope she still does. The street is empty as I walk through the dark and I'm glad. I have literally no idea what could be lurking out here. God being a sex slave really cuts you off to the rest of the world. Anyway, I digress. The street is empty and after awhile seems kind of lonely. I miss being surrounded by the denizens of the dark. God, we had some fun times.

As I get closer to Medusa's home, I see statues all over the street and I know she's back on her bullshit. I'd be worried If I wasn't a woman. Some of the statues look like the monsters that the angel of destruction turned the first borns into. I step around one and notice her home is completely gone. I'm stunned for a moment. She was my only lead. I hope her and the baby made it out of the house okay. It looks like one of those creatures ripped right through it. I continue walking right past the carnage and start to look for churches. He's probably in one of those right. I mean he's friggin Jesus. Where else would he be. My hopes are dashed yet again as every church I find also looks to be destroyed. Like the monsters were targeting places of the lord. I mean it's possible. They were created by Lucifer's child.

With nothing else to do I keep wandering the city. It truly looks like a hellscape. Vacant and crumbling, like a war forced everyone to evacuate. I expected to at least find some people. Maybe creatures. But there's nothing. Soon the sun will rise, and as much as I'd like to see it, there's this odd push inside of me to hide from it. Too tired to mull it out I go inside of the next abandoned looking house in the neighborhood I'm walking through. Since moving in with Lucy I've slept through the day and partied all night. My body begs for rest now and I oblige it. The door to the house is hanging ajar and I close it behind me. This house is trashed and actually looks like somebody died here. I just hope there's still a bed. I stagger upstairs and fall into the first room. I'd underestimated how tired the crash from Jesus blood would eventually make me. The room still has a bed, oddly made up with what looks like a clean blanket, but I shrug that off as I collapse onto it and fall asleep. When I wake up later, the sun is bright in the room from a hole in the wall next to the bed I hadn't paid attention to when I'd pretty much passed out. And I can't move my legs. As I start to reach down and touch them, I realize I'm handcuffed to the headboard.

"I don't remember consenting to this," I mumble.

"Shut your mouth harlot. What are you doing in my house?"

I look over at the male voice and see a middle-aged man with a grimy beard clutching a shotgun and aiming it at me. "Don't slut shame me bro. You're the kinky one that handcuffed me to the bed."

"What are you doing in my house?"

"Just looking for a place to sleep, what the fuck did you do to my legs?"

"Nothing."

"Bullshit, I can't move them," I say as I wiggle and try to get movement from my bottom half. They feel like they did right after Lucy threw Logan's semen on me and I realize my legs are laying in a patch of sunlight and I'm assuming they're stone. "Fuck." How long is that going to last, I wonder, but now that I come to think of it, I realize I've never seen Logan or Lathan out during the day, and I wonder if this is why. Did I turn myself into a gargoyle when I drank Christ's blood?

"Look, I'm real hot, could you maybe move my legs out of the sun. Please."

The man lowers the gun a little and he looks like he might. "No tricks," he says.

"Only treats," I can't help but say.

"What?" he snaps, raising the gun back up.

"Kidding, kidding, Jesus' calm down. I'm sweating my tits off please move them."

The man edges toward me and pushes my legs with the barrel of his gun. They don't move, but I can hear that it in fact they have turned to stone. He looks suspicious before tucking the gun under his arm and moving my legs with some effort out of the sun. Once it's out of the light I can feel life returning to my limbs. I move my arm to shake his hand forgetting its handcuffed and feel the metal snap. We both glanced at it stunned. I recover myself before he can raise the gun and I fling myself out of the bed and slam into him. He falls backward and I stumble forward out of the room and sprint down the stairs. I almost rip open the front door when I remember the light will turn me to stone and turn toward the back of the house. I hope to find an entrance to a basement, but unfortunately, I just find the backdoor. The gun goes off behind me and I feel the bullet hit me in the back, the buckshot spattering me in several places. Aghast I look down at my stomach expecting to see blood pooling from an exit wound, but there is nothing. I hear the pellets hit the floor and the man gasp. Turns out being a gargoyle is really fucking cool.

"Wha . . . what the hell are you," he gasps, his voice quivering.

"A denizen of the night." God, I feel powerful.

"Don't, don't kill me."

I stroke my chin appearing pensive. "I'll let you live If . . ."

"If? If what?"

"If you can tell me where to find Jesus."

"Look around, god has abandoned us."

"Not god, Jesus. I haven't seen him in a year, but he's here." I hope. What's to say he hasn't moved on. Why should he stay in the epicenter of his second coming?

"Why you looking for Jesus in a hail Satan t-shirt?"

"I like to play the field. You sure you ain't seen Jesus? It'd be a shame to have to kill you."

He steps back. "Wait a minute. He's not exactly Jesus, but the guy who runs the soup kitchen calls himself JC."

"And you never put two and two together. Where the fuck is, he getting the food if he's not Jesus? Lucy controls all the food."

"Huh. I guess it makes sense. Can I go?"

I shrug. "I mean I can't leave till its dark."

He backs away until he makes it to the front door then he bolts. With a sigh I sit down to wait out the rest of the day. I'm not sure sleeping would be safe after what just happened.

After dark I find "JC" in his soup kitchen. A line of grimy looking people wraps around the block. I stand across the street watching him ladle soup into bowls, yet the pot never empties. And somehow the streetlights above him still work and this section of town doesn't look as bad as the rest. I recognize him straight away as Jesus, but he's giving off serious Strega Nona vibes. I wait until the line is done before I step forward into the streetlight.

"Got enough for one more?" I ask.

"There's always enough for one more," he says without looking up from his pot.

"Even for a sinner like me, Jesus."

He finally looks up from his pot. "Let he who is without sin cast the first stone."

"That would be you."

He smiles. "We are all to blame for what we have now."

I'd like to believe that, I really would. But he was laying blameless on a slab of stone. I did this. I cursed the world and damned myself.

"You saved me. Why should I condemn you for that?"

"If you're that far into my head, then you know Lucy tried to turn me to stone."

"How very Judas of her," he says as he ladles soup. "But she is owed the next six years."

I accept the bowl because I am a little hungry. "I don't care what that bitch is owed. I'm going to take it from her."

"My hands are tied."

"There must be something we can do."

"Not I. But there is a being far older who would love to take the Earth back."

"Done. Where are they?"

"You sure you know what you're doing?" he asks.

"Revenge," I say before taking a bite of the soup. It's actually pretty good.

"You know you could just walk away," he says.

"And go where?"

He opens his arms with a smile.

"No thanks, you're a little too pure for me."

"Alright, if you're sure this is what you want then follow me."

I put the partially eaten bowl down and followed him into the dark. I need this more than food. All I asked for was honesty and transparency. Instead, the crazy bitch tried to encase me in stone so she could look better. So much for mutual respect.

Jesus leads me through town to the graveyard. A half-moon bathes it in an eerie light as we wade through waist high grass that's swishing in the wind. I keep my focus on my feet, afraid to trip over a hidden headstone. The cemetery is the saddest thing I've seen since leaving Lucy. There's no one to care for this final resting place.

Jesus leads me to a mausoleum. "Last chance to back out."

"Is there a fucking vampire in there?" God if the answer to this is a vampire I'm going to be pissed.

"No," he says as he opens it and steps in. "Something more primal."

Jesus pushes the sarcophagus aside and I see a set of stairs descending into the dark. My gargoyle eyes make it easier to see in the dark and I descend first. I hear Jesus footsteps follow. At the base of the stairs is a circular room. Seven stone beings are set into the wall. Two poles stand waist high in the middle of the room with balls on top. Jesus walks over to them and grabs the balls. I smell the tang of blood as spikes come out of them and inject into his hands. He barely winces, but I suppose that's because he's had worse. His blood fills channels in the floor and go into the beings. I hear the crack of stone as they separate from the wall and large wings stretch out behind them. They look like what I would expect a Gargoyle would. All seven fly up the stairs and disappear. The spikes release Jesus and he sags to the floor. I help him to his feet and up the stairs. As we exit the mausoleum, I see the winged creatures flying up into the sky.

"Where are they going?" I ask.

"To get her."

"Who?"

"Mother."

The beings soon disappear in the dark, but I keep staring wondering where this mother person could be. A bright light erupts in the sky and I see it plummet towards the Earth.

"There," he points. "There she is."

His voice sounds like he's in awe. She falls from the heavens, a bright fiery light and lands outside of town.

"Go to her," he says.

"What about you?"

"I just need some wine and communion crackers and I'll be right as rain."

Out of nowhere he's got a bottle of wine in his hand, so I ease him down and go back in the mausoleum. The sun will be up soon. I'll find her at nightfall. In the meantime, I find a quiet corner and sleep. When the sun goes down, I find that Jesus has left. Part of me wonders what we just did, but I guess I'll find out firsthand in a bit. I walk toward the place where the mother fell. As I move, I go past Jesus' soup line. A sense of fear has settled over the crowd and Jesus looks at me like I told you so. I ignore him. Maybe if he had gotten revenge we wouldn't be in this predicament. I can't turn the other cheek like him. Lucy will pay.

Walking into the middle of nowhere takes what feels like forever. Especially since excitement spurs me onward. I honestly can't wait to meet her. And I can't wait for her to fuck up Lucy's life. Trees surround me now, but there are no night noises. Almost like nature is holding its breath. I hear what appears to be chanting and alter my course just enough to see what it is. I can make out the words, 'worship on your knees. Worship with your tongue.' The chanting grows in intensity the closer I get, and I stumble out of the trees into perhaps the oddest scene and that's saying something.

A naked woman lays on a slab of stone. People sit with their backs to her on their knees. Their eyes are white and unseeing, and I realize the chant is coming from them. Vines stretch from the woman skin and appear to be attached at the base of the people's skulls. A vine snakes through the grass and implants in the back of my head as well. Then she's inside my head. Beautiful and perfect and I feel the chant in my bones. I drop to my knees. She must be worshiped.

Another vine slides up my leg and disappears into my pants. I feel it caress my clit as it moves toward my vagina, and I spread my legs. The vine enters me, slowly at first but then impales me. I cry out in ecstasy. It's been two whole days since I've been fucked, and it feels phenomenal. I rock against the vine as it slides in and out of me. I'm in a frenzy, I need more. I scream the word in my head, and she smiles. The vine slides in one more time and as I cum it implants a seed in my womb. The vine withdraws slick and moist and returns inside of her vagina. The vine releases from the back of my neck and I feel her arms catch me. It feels so natural to be cradled in her arms. I look around and see that the others have been released as well, but they are all dried husks. Like she drained the life from them.

I lay in her arms and look up at the trees around us. The stone creatures sit in the branches watching us. Mother smooth's my hair out of my face. I've never been held like this in my entire life and I feel like this must be what love is. Mother holds something to my lips, and I open them. She puts it in my mouth, and I swallow. I have to feed the baby. Whatever it is. Never thought I'd ever want one, but that's how badly I want to get back at Lucy. If this whatever it is can do that, I'll feed it and birth it so it can. As we lay there, time disappears. All there is, is the feeling of her arms around me. And then there's snakes. I don't know if she calls them or if they're attracted by what I carry inside, but most of them slither up inside of me and are never seen again. Mother says the baby is eating them. It's designed to feed on serpents. They scramble to get inside and some of them I eat. The baby is growing and it's going to eat Lucy. The snakes constantly slither over me and Mother. In my mouth, up my vagina, and my belly grows. When it is so swollen, I can barely see over it, the creatures in the trees swoop down and pick me up. They carry me through the night to Lucy's palace. In through the door and into the throne room. Lucy watches curiously as they gingerly set me on the floor, my lower half pointed at her. Her body spasms and she turns into a giant serpent then phases back to her human form.

"What the fuck," Lucy says as she eyes me like she has never seen me before. "What the fuck was that."

"The swallower of serpents," I mumble. I can feel how hungry my child is. It's ravenous and the only thing that will satiate it is her. The queen of serpents.

Lucy moves toward me like she's pulled by a magnet. Her body moves from human to serpent and back again as she struggles to pull herself backward. I feel my baby pushing out of me in an attempt to eat her. Its mouth comes out first and I look between my legs to see a big round opening. Lucy is flailing trying to not get sucked in and failing. Her snake form finally takes over and she slides across the floor into the baby's mouth. Before it swallows her, her head turns human and she's looking up at me from between my knees.

"What the fuck did I ever do to you?"

"You tried to turn me to stone. Now we're even."

With a shocked look Lucy is sucked into my baby's mouth and it slides out of my vagina to lay on the floor. It has four legs, a vacuous mouth, and hairless skin. I gaze down at it, no motherly instinct to suckle it at my breast or hug it. The baby did what is was designed to do. Rid the world of a snake. And I am grateful, but no more than that.

"Now what?" I ask.

Mother stands above me with a smile. "We remake the world."

Did you love *Wacky John*? Then you should read *Boken Girl Broken World*[1] by Eady H!

[2]

Six Dead. Don't go out at night.

Six months ago the What's your name killer brutally murdered six women and marked a seventh. But before he could complete his work the dead rose from their graves and took over the Earth. Believing him dead the seventh victim tries to move on but is tortured by her own mind. As she spirals into darkness she teeters on the edge of becoming what she fears most.

---

1. https://books2read.com/u/mv91aV

2. https://books2read.com/u/mv91aV

Also by Eady H

Double Creature Feature
Double Creature Feature

Valoryn Universe
The End of Creation Enforcement

Standalone
The Earth Swallows
Where the Dark Things Are
Two-Bit Detective
Boken Girl Broken World
Wacky John